SHATTERED

THE SECRET LIFE OF TRYSTAN SCOTT

VOL. 4

H.M. WARD

www.SexyAwesomeBooks.com

Laree Bailey Press

Laree Bailey Press
First Print Edition: September 2013
ISBN-13: 978-0615883007

SHATTERED

THE SECRET LIFE OF TRYSTAN SCOTT

VOL. 4

shat-ter: to violently break something into pieces

CHAPTER 1

~MARI~

I run. I run out the front door of my house sobbing. I don't know what I think or what I need. I just know that I want Trystan, but when I get to his house, something's wrong. When Trystan pulls the door open, it seems like he is going to walk out, which is strange since he's not wearing a shirt and his hair is damp. I glance at his face—his blue eyes are wild. They're too big, like he has no idea what to do, like I'm the last person he expected on his doorstep.

Trystan hesitates. He looks over his shoulder with panic in his eyes. He tells me to leave in a rush of air. I can hardly make out the word. My heart is pounding. My skin prickles. Something is wrong, but I don't understand. Before I have a chance to ask, someone slams into Trystan. The door snaps shut as their bodies collide and fall into the wall.

I scream. My hands fly to my face as the sound rips out of the back of my throat. Someone is hurting him. Now it makes sense. Now the look on his face, the fear in his eyes, means something. Trystan was going to run out the front door, but I was standing there blocking his way. If he tried to run past, whoever is fighting with Trystan could have come after me instead.

Trystan threw himself in the middle. He knew someone was behind him.

Glancing around frantically, I try to figure out what to do. I'm tiny. I can't do anything, but I know what I saw. Someone is hurting Trystan. I pull my cell phone from my pocket and call 911. I'm not even sure what I'm saying. I repeat myself and say the name of the condo unit one more time. They ask me too many questions. They try to keep me in place, but I can't just stand there. I put the phone down without hanging up. They can find me.

That's when things get worse. I hear Trystan's voice through the front window. It's a strangled yelp and then a crash. Glass shatters inside the house. Horrors are taking place behind that door. My heart thumps in my chest so furiously that I think it might crack my ribs. My muscles tense. Every part of me knows that I'll get my ass kicked—maybe worse—if I walk through that door, but I have to. I can't leave him in there. I can't wait for the police. Trystan needs me. Someone's hurting him.

I can't just stand here and cower. But I have nothing to fight with. I glance around and see a busted up brick in the parking lot. I run and grab it. Then, I do the stupidest thing I've ever done in my entire life—I open the door and go inside.

The sight makes me stop in my tracks. My mouth gapes open. A man in a white dress shirt has Trystan by the throat and is pressing him into the wall. Trystan's hands are wrapped tightly around the man's wrists. Every muscle in Trystan's body is corded tight, like they could snap at any second. His face is a mixture of pain and terror, and is the wrong color. He can't breathe. Trystan doesn't see me. The other man doesn't hear me. He's screaming at Trystan, blaming him for something that I can't understand. Every time the man screams, he shoves Trystan back into the wall, harder and harder, choking him.

Rage courses through my veins. My muscles tense and I don't think. I feel the rock burning a hole in my hand. I feel the pull toward the man's back, as if the broken brick wants to collide with his head. I launch myself across the room and swing my arm. My hand comes down hard and the brick slams into the man's head. But, I realize my mistake too late. I'm too short, too weak. I didn't hit him hard enough.

Instead of falling to the ground, the man drops Trystan to the floor and rounds on me. His eyes burn like acid, overflowing with hatred. I know I'm going to die. The way he looks at me, the way his hands float up so slowly, makes every hair on my body stand on end. I slide one shoe back. My senses are all hypersensitive, but it doesn't help. I know what he's going to do. I see him coming toward me, slowly fixating his focus on my neck. I know he wants to snap me like a twig. My lips are parted, but I can't speak. Someone has stolen my voice.

"What the fuck gives you the right to attack me in my own home?" His voice is like gravel and nails. Venom is laced thickly through every word. His shoulders are hunched forward like he's ready to pounce and bury me in the ground.

My heart hammers harder. I don't understand. I blink, even though I don't want to take my eyes off the man. "You were hurting him." The words come out of my mouth in a huff of air as though he's already choking me.

"It's none of your damn business what I do to him." The man's jaw shifts back and forth. He steps toward me and grabs my wrist. I scream and he shoves me back into the wall. I claw at my arm, at that one wrist that he has pinned, but I'm not strong enough.

The man hisses in my face, "He's my kid, not yours. I should break your hand for this. You came into my home and attacked me. No one would blame me, you know. No one would know what happened here. They'd say you were lucky that I didn't shoot you." He twists my wrist slowly, twisting it farther and farther.

My heart pounds frantically, as pain shoots up my arm. I try to pull away from him, but I can't. I scratch at his hand, the one holding me, and kick his shins, but he just laughs. It's like I'm a fly. I can't do anything to stop him. Fear makes my body shake. He smiles like he's enjoying hurting me, like he'll really do it.

I freak out. My brain snaps. Trystan is battered and bloody on the floor and this lunatic is his father. This is the person responsible. Before I know what I'm doing, my mouth lands on his shoulder and I bite. He screams and throws me back. The floor hits me hard and I roll onto my side. There's no time—there's no time to run or crawl away. Before I can blink, his foot connects with my stomach. Pain shoots through me as tears burst from my eyes. A raw scream rips from my throat. I try to curl into a ball, but the man doesn't stop. It's like he can't stop, like he has to finish this. I scream louder as the foot comes at me again, but it doesn't connect.

Trystan is yelling, his voice is mangled, but I still understand him. "Don't touch her!" He's standing. There are angry marks around his neck and his lip is split. A trail of blood runs down his cheek. That wound from the other day, the one that Tucker was upset about, opened up.

Tucker. Tucker knew something was wrong. My eyes dart to Trystan. His dad has been beating the shit out of him. I didn't know. Horror washes over me in a frigid wave. How did I not know?

Trystan's dad has a strange look on his face. I get to my feet even though my middle feels like it's been smashed to bits. Trystan stands between us. His shoulders are tense, corded with muscle, ready to fight. I don't breathe. I can't. Everything happens so quickly, but it feels like forever, like we're moving through a vat of Vaseline.

Trystan's dad takes a swing at his son. Angry words come pouring out of his mouth and his fist follows. Trystan remains between us, dodges the hit, and swings his arm straight up. Trystan's fist connects under his dad's jaw. The punch is solid. The man's bones make a cracking sound before he gets a strange look on his face and falls backwards. His body hits the floor.

Trystan stands over his father, breathing hard, his fingers still clenched into a fist. Neither of us moves. Trystan's shaking, looking at his hand like he's some kind of monster. When he turns back to me, I nearly die. His expression is horrible. All the anguish is plainly painted across his face for me to see.

We both stare at each other for a second. It feels like time stops, but in a bad way. I finally remember I have feet and lunge at him, throwing myself into his arms. Trystan's chest is slick, covered in sweat. I feel every muscle in his body as he wraps his arms around me. He buries his face in my hair and we stay like that until the lights and voices tear us apart. Trystan releases me and looks up confused. Their words sound like far away echoes. They say to drop to the floor, to let go of me. Neither of us moves. We both shiver as the men run at us. One pulls me from Trystan, while the other knocks him to the floor and pulls his arms behind his back.

A police officer speaks to me. "Are you all right? Are you the one who called? Miss…" he continues to talk, but I'm shaking. I can't understand why they're hurting Trystan. I can't understand anything.

I blurt out, "He didn't hurt me! That man did. What are you doing?" I try to pull away from the cop, but he keeps me back. More police are there. Another cop car. They say that I should calm down. They ask my name, my parent's names. They want to know what happened, if I'm all right. But I can't speak, they don't listen when I tell them that Trystan is hurt. They pull Trystan away from me and I can't see him. It feels like there's a foot on my chest and I can't breathe.

CHAPTER 2

~TRYSTAN~

Something inside of him snapped this time. When Trystan saw Mari fall and his father's foot connect with her stomach, his brain broke. Red hot rage ran behind his eyes, blinding him. Before Trystan knew what happened, his father was on the floor. He remembers the steps toward his dad. He remembers the way it felt when his fist collided with the old man's jaw. Maybe dad deserved it. Maybe, but that isn't the emotion rolling over his skin. Trystan looks at his hand, still clenched tight. That fist. Oh god. He didn't want to fight back. Fighting back makes it worse. Fighting back makes him like his father. Trystan's stomach twists as he stares at nothing.

After a moment, he sees her—Mari. She moves toward him. Shame covers him like a thick blanket. He didn't defend her fast enough. He didn't prevent this. He should have. When Mari falls against him, Trystan pulls her to him, touching her back and lacing his fingers through her hair. He saw the kick and knows how much she hurts. Trystan is careful not to make it worse, but he doesn't want to let go. Closing his eyes, he buries his face in her hair and breathes. It seems like hours pass this way.

His life is so fucked up, so far beyond repair—and Mari walked straight into it. She saw him when he opened the door, but she didn't run. Mari came inside. She must have done something after he blacked out. The last thing Trystan remembers is his father's fingers around his throat and the liquid fire filling his lungs.

Then, Trystan opened his eyes and the world was on its side. Mari was on the floor. It was too much. Trystan was too late. He didn't save her. He walked her into this mess, led her straight into it.

Mari's hands are warm and hold onto him tightly. She doesn't hold back. It isn't until the cops arrive that they part, and it isn't willingly. Before Trystan knows what's happening, he's forced to the floor with a knee in his back. They say things to him, but the pain is making it hard to focus. He can't swallow. His entire throat burns and aches at the same time. It's like his neck was in a vice, but it wasn't. It was in his father's hands.

They pull Trystan up and drag him into the kitchen. The wall blocks his view of Mari. Anger is coursing so wildly through his body that he can barely control it. The cops ask him questions, but he can't really speak. Each word is like a nail through his throat. The only things he can manage is, "It's not her fault. I did this." They shove paper at him. Trystan knows better than to write anything down. He shakes his head.

"Don't be a dumbass kid. Write down what happened." The cop pushes the paper back at Trystan, but he doesn't take it. "You're old man beat you one too many times. We know this story kid. The girl showed up and tried to help. Things got out of hand. I know how this goes. Tell us something." But Trystan is quiet.

The cop glances through the doorway to the cops in the other room. He shakes his head once, and turns his attention back to Trystan. Another cop comes into the room. He's shaking his head, like he can't believe Trystan's so stupid.

"Are you a minor, kid?" the new cop asks. Trystan shakes his head and wishes he didn't. It makes his head throb more. He mutters curse words under his breathe and looks back at Trystan's dad who is still lying on the floor.

A few minutes later the paramedics arrive. Trystan doesn't want them to look at him, but the cops insist. There's no way to pay for this, but they look him over anyway.

They tell Trystan that he'll be all right. They tell him that his father is awake and unharmed, but they are taking him in anyway. They repeat a question, "You sure you didn't pass out? Not even for a second?"

Trystan mouths *no.* He lies. He isn't going to the damn emergency room. Trystan knows exactly where he's going as soon as the paramedics leave.

"Kid, we're going to have to bring you to the jail if you don't go with them. Blacking out would be normal. It's nothing to do with how much of a man you are." The cop looks at him. He doesn't understand. It isn't blacking out. It's that his private life is suddenly exposed. All those years of misery are out in the open. The only thing Trystan wanted was to get through the next couple of months and then go out on his own. This wasn't part of the plan.

Mari appears in the doorway. "I'm not pressing charges." Trystan perks up in his chair, but the cop places a hand on his shoulder to keep him in place. There are two officers with Mari, walking her out to the car. She screamed the words as she passed by.

Trystan says, "But her father will."

"Smart boy. Come on. Let's get going. You're going to have a long night." The cop gestures for Trystan to stand and hold out his wrists. Cold metal bites into Trystan's skin when the handcuffs tighten. He blinks slowly, wondering how he ended up with this life.

CHAPTER 3

~MARI~

Tear stains streak my cheeks. When the cop car pulls up in front of my parent's house, I nearly die. One of the officers goes ahead to the door, while the other one fishes me out of the backseat.

"They aren't home," I say.

The two cops look at me. They're both young with no

wrinkles around their eyes. One has dark skin and the other one is so pale that he's practically glowing. They're like a law enforcement ying-yang.

The pasty guy asks, "Where are they?"

"Work," I say. They're always at work. And if these guys call them, I'm going to get my ass handed to me. It doesn't matter that it isn't my fault. "My dad's a surgeon. My mom's a nurse. Is there any way you could take care of this with them in the morning?" They both shake their heads. I reach for the door and stick in the key. "Fine, come inside." I keep talking as I walk in. They follow me. Their heads swivel on their shoulders as they take in the house. Everyone does that. It's too posh, too pretty. It's a status symbol in the extreme.

"Do you want coffee or something?"

"No, thank you, Miss," the cop with the super-tan says. His name is Marcello. I squint to read it on his chest. "We'll just wait for your parents. What time do you expect them?"

"In the morning. They both work the night shift." I quickly add, "And if you call them, and I'm not dead, I will be when they get home." I can't say more. I hope to God that they understand what I mean and take me seriously.

The pasty cop furrows his brow. He steps toward me. "Is someone hurting you here?"

I say nothing. I just stare at them. No one is hurting me. No one is ever here. It's not like what Trystan was enduring. My God. My stomach clenches thinking about him, about the pain in his eyes. He hid it from me all these years. There were times he seemed off, but I couldn't figure him out. Now I know why. I feel sick.

Pressing my lips together, I ask, "What'd you do with Trystan?"

"He's been taken in for questioning. They should let him go, because of what it is. You're the wild card in this equation. Your parents need to be notified. If they want to press charges, we'll be forced to comply."

"What does that mean?" I ask looking at both of them. "Why would they press charges?"

Marcello takes a deep breath. His eyes shift and he looks at his partner. Neither of them wants to tell me, but they both know the answer. "Just be glad things didn't get worse, okay. And stay away from that complex. There's some low-life scum in that part of town."

"Trystan's not like that," I say, automatically defending him. "He's a good guy. His dad beat the shit out him."

Marcello doesn't want to say it. His eyes shift to the side and then back to me. "Listen, kid. Guys like that don't get second chances. His dad may have been the one that messed him up, but there's no saving him. You understand? There's nothing left to save. He's already gone. Stay away from guys like that if you want to be happy."

The cop stares at me like I'm his little sister, like he's remembering something. He blinks and looks away. His partner is at the door. They're leaving to find my parents. I hope to God that my parents aren't at work—that somehow they fail to be notified—because I know how this will end. My throat constricts and my heart pounds harder. I say nothing else. They nod and leave. Once again, I am alone.

The next morning, my parents sit across the table from me. They eat breakfast like nothing happened last night. They don't even talk about it. It isn't until I stand to leave that my father asks my mother about the lawyer.

I stop and turn with my plate in my hands. I'm worried that they're going to press charges against Trystan. "Lawyer for what?"

Daddy shoots daggers at me with his eyes. "For what? Oh, let's see. First of all there was that assault you were involved in with Brie and then there was the incident last night." His jaw twitches. I know he wants to scream at me until his eyes get too big for his head and that vein in his temple swells to spaghetti size.

"She had nothing to do with the incident last night. The officer said—" Mother is kind. She tries to defend me for once, but Daddy cuts her off.

"The officer was being polite. He didn't want to say that our daughter was with a derelict and his drunken father, doing God knows what, when things got out of hand." Daddy gives Mom a stern look and she lowers her head and goes back to her eggs. My heart falls inside my chest. I wish she'd defend me. Just once.

When Daddy resumes his rant, his voice is tense, clipped. "I'm not pressing charges. It'll cost more than it's worth." I hear *it'll cost more than you're worth.* It rings crystal clear in my head, like he actually said it. He looks up at me and asks, "Tell me, Mari—do you intend to throw away your life on someone so utterly beneath you, or do you intend to make something of yourself? Actions like this have consequences and from where I stand, you're throwing away your life. You're nothing but a goddamn waste."

His words cut me in two. I don't know what I expected him to say but that wasn't it. I move robotically to the sink and set my plate down. My chest constricts and turns cold. My eyes don't blink, they look but they don't see. I don't see Daddy go back to his breakfast like he wished me well today. I don't see my mother cowering, doing nothing to prevent his words from stabbing me in the heart. I've done nothing to warrant this from him, yet, this is my treatment. I'm an inconvenience. He makes that abundantly clear.

I'm a bill.

I'm an expense.

I'm an adverse risk, one that he would have rather lived without.

CHAPTER 4

~TRYSTAN~

The police don't know what to do with him. Trystan is too old or too young. The cops don't want to throw him in jail, but they haven't released him yet, either. Trystan sits in the police station after questioning that took too long. He didn't say much. There wasn't much to say.

The police station is busy even though it's getting late. It seems like the later it gets, the more stupid people become. Trystan is sitting in an old beat up wooden chair by the detective's desk. The cop sits next to him filling out paperwork, not saying much. Trystan's gaze is carefully placed on the floor where it can't attract trouble. His arms are folded over his chest and he's slumped back in his seat. There isn't anything that he wouldn't give to be somewhere else. This trip, this whole damn night, is going to ruin his shot at the army. Trystan stares at his toe, the once-white part of his Converse, as he thinks that plan was shot to hell anyway. Mari loves him. Mari wants to be with him.

And now this.

Trystan rubs his hands over his face and back through his hair. He stretches and looks over at the cop. "Can I go?" He's polite. It's a stupid question. After everything that happened, Trystan's sure they won't release him.

"Not yet, kid. Let me finish this and you can sign it. If the girl's family presses charges, we'll deal with it then. I don't want to throw you in a cell with the guys that are in there tonight. Too much shit has happened. They'll rip you apart before you even get a chance to turn around." The cop has a wrinkled dress shirt on. His tie is loosened around his neck. His face is covered in wrinkles and his skin weathered like old leather. There are too many creases and he has that smoky smell that comes from lighting up too many times each day. The cop doesn't look up at Trystan.

This is the first time anyone told him what was going on. Since they dragged him into the station, no one said anything to him. Trystan doesn't want to ask, but he can't help it. "Did they say if they're going to press charges?"

The cop nods, not looking up from his paperwork. "Not yet, but she's a minor. They'll probably talk to their lawyer in the morning and we'll hear back then." He glances up at Trystan and points a pen at the string of bruises blossoming around Trystan's neck. "From the look of things, it could have been a lot worse. You're lucky."

Trystan laughs. The sound is so bitter that he can taste it. "If that was lucky—"

The cop cuts him off. He looks straight at Trystan and narrows his eyes. "Damn right, it was lucky. Lucky she showed up. Lucky your old man didn't break her ribs. Lucky you're still breathing. You were lucky, Trystan. No one else stepped in. That parking lot was filled with people. They all minded their own business and let your dad strangle you. That girl saved your ass." His old eyes hold Trystan's for a moment and his expression softens. "If you've got some family you can stay with until you graduate, do it. These things don't end well. Once you pass that point, once you fight back, there's just going to be more of it." Trystan holds the cop's gaze for a second and nods.

Trystan gets what the detective is saying. *Don't go home.*

Trystan slides down further in the seat. His arms are flexed tightly across his chest with his head lowered. It's the only way to hide the marks on his neck. He swallows hard and waits, thinking. Too many thoughts, too many images flood his mind. Everything in his life sucks, everything expect Mari.

When Trystan thinks about what she did, how she raced in like she wasn't the least bit afraid—oh God. If there was a rewind button on life, Trystan would press it. He would go back and delete the whole thing. If he'd never went home, this wouldn't have happened. As it is, it kills him that Mari was hurt and he couldn't stop it.

There are too many things wrong with his life, too many things that he can't fix.

———

A noise startles Trystan awake. He rolls over on the old couch and flinches. His shirt is on the floor and he's wearing nothing but his jeans and a tattered blanket from the prop bin. When Trystan had nowhere to go, he decided to break into the school and sleep in the prop room. No one comes down there early in the morning, which is confusing him now.

Trystan blinks again and yawns. A pair of brown eyes and soft dark hair comes into focus. "Mari?" he asks, still half asleep. He wonders if he's dreaming. Trystan blinks again, but his throat is still aching. It feels like his body was ripped apart last night and reassembled. Add to that the shame he's feeling and Trystan can barely breathe.

Mari reaches for him and smoothes her hand across his cheek. Her touch is warm, gentle. "Did you sleep here?" Her eyes slide over his chest and then back up to his face.

Trystan stretches and sits up, letting the blanket fall from his body. He really doesn't want to answer. It isn't that he doesn't trust Mari, it's that he wishes that part of his life didn't exist. But, after last night he owes her. Trystan rubs the sleep from his eyes and says, "Yeah. I had to. I couldn't go home."

"What happened last night after I left? I tried to stay, but they wouldn't let me do anything. The police treated me like a child. It…" her gaze is on the side of his face. She lets out a sigh and closes her eyes for a second. When she reopens them again, Mari looks at the same spot on the floor as Trystan. They both have that vacant gaze.

"I was worried about you." She bumps his knees with hers.

"I'm fine," Trystan says, but deep inside he's not fine. Somehow Mari got sucked into his private hell, and that makes it worse. Trystan couldn't stop it. When he finally passed out on the couch last night, the whole nightmare unfolded again and again as he dreamed. That's the problem with his life, there is no escaping it, not even in sleep. Trystan glances past Mari, looking for his shirt. "What about you? Did your Dad…"

Mari stirs and sees his shirt. She reaches for it and hands it to him. Trystan pulls the fabric over his head as she speaks, but her eyes lift to his neck and lock there. She can't tear her gaze away. "Dad doesn't listen to me. He doesn't hit me, but sometimes I think he will. Oh God, Trystan. Why didn't you tell me? I had no idea—"

"There's a reason why you had no idea. I love you, Mari, I really do—but I can't talk about this. It isn't something that I want to share. I'm completely horrified that you walked into it. I'm horrified that he hurt you. I…" Trystan's jaw drops open and for the first time since it happened, he really looks at Mari. He meets her gaze and holds it. She's his refuge. Mari is his glue, his balm, his other half. Her brown eyes are wide. Her narrow fingers are gripped tightly in front of her waist, like she thinks she did something wrong. "I just want to get past it and now I can't even hide it. Everyone is going to see my neck and know."

Mari is wearing an oversized flannel shirt. Without a word, she unbuttons it, revealing the cami beneath. Trystan doesn't realize what she's doing until she holds out the flannel to him. "Take it. It has a collar. And I have access to the stage make-up. That will cover up the marks in front. No one will know. Everything will be okay." Even as she says it, Trystan knows

Mari doesn't believe it. There's a look in her eye, but he doesn't press her about it. Instead he nods and takes the shirt, grateful.

Mari changes the subject and talks about other things while she dabs thick, cold, goopy, foundation on his neck. This will work. It covers everything. Her fingers are so soft and work so fast. Trystan waits until she stops talking and asks, "What made you come here this morning? School doesn't start for another hour or more." Part of him thinks that she was looking for him. The other part thinks something happened, something with her dad.

Mari's shoulders tense. She stands taller and her eyes dart away. He's right. Fuck, he didn't want to be right. She licks her lips and finishes covering up his mangled neck. "I had to get out of my house. You know how it is."

"Yeah, I know." He's quiet for a moment.

Mari is wearing one of those cami's with the lace at the top. It hugs her body, closely fitting to every curve. His eyes drink her in. In the back of Trystan's mind, he knows that he's going to lose her. Life isn't fair and he knows that, but losing her so soon is unbearable.

Mari's dark hair falls down her back in a cascade of thick curls. They sway and fall over her shoulder as she works. Mari moves around him, not feeling his eyes on her skin as she picks up the make-up and puts it back in the kit. Trystan feels so torn. He needs her, but she'd be so much better off without him. Trystan has nothing to offer her. He only brings pain and shame. He swallows hard, trying to ignore the guilt that's choking him.

When Mari turns around, she has a soft smile on her lips. She isn't afraid of him. She doesn't pity him. Mari acts like Trystan is the same guy he was yesterday, before she learned his secret. She sits down next to him and helps him pull her shirt on. It was too big on her, but it's about the right size for him. She buttons it up, a few of the top buttons she leaves open, and smiles at him.

Mari places her hand over his heart and says, "No one will know."

Their eyes lock. A rush of emotion floods through him. Trystan feels too much. After everything that happened, he just wants to hold onto her and never let go. Acting on the urge, Trystan leans in and gathers Mari in his arms and holds her tight. She winces as he does it, which makes him let go. "You're hurt."

Trystan's blue gaze slips over the cami. He doesn't see anything. Slowly, he inches his hand toward the hem of her shirt. Mari is very still, her dark eyes tracking his hands as he takes the bottom of her cami and slowly slides it up. An angry purple mark mars her perfectly pale skin. He can't breathe. Things can't be like this. She's hurt because of him. He shouldn't do this. He shouldn't be here with her and he sure as hell shouldn't be touching her, but he can't stop. It's still early. No one is here. Trystan could slide his fingers along her soft skin and press his lips to hers. She could take him away from here with a taste of those lips. Trystan could be higher than high in a heartbeat if he just leaned in and kissed her.

Mari's eyes drift to his lips. His hands are still on her shirt, his fingers are so close to her skin that it aches not to touch her. Mari takes a jagged breath and looks up at him. Her eyes are molten chocolate. They shimmer with golden heat. The way she looks at him makes Trystan's heart beat harder. Suddenly, he's hot all over. His body is responding to her. He wants to lean in. Trystan wants to be with her, but he doesn't move.

Trystan's lips are a breath from Mari's. The stay like that too long, impossibly long. Lingering thoughts tease him, telling him to take what he needs—that she'll let him—that Mari needs him just as much. But he can't. He can't drag her into this more than he already has. Guilt juts up between them like a wall.

Trystan blinks and breaks their gaze. He turns his face away from Mari without explanation. He sucks in air and runs his hands through his hair and down the back of his neck.

She deserves so much more.

CHAPTER 5

~MARI~

When Trystan pulls away, it feels like my lungs have been ripped out of my throat. I don't understand why he does it. My heart races frantically, and won't calm down. Trystan bends forward and lowers his head like he's praying. He doesn't look up right away. I want to take him in my arms and fix this, but I know I can't. There are too many things bottled up inside of him, too many thoughts that I don't know. So, I do the only thing that I know to do.

I stand up and smooth my shirt back into place. My middle is still sore as hell, but I'd rather die than pass up the chance to have Trystan's hands on me.

"Come on, Scott," I say, grabbing a pillow off the couch. The thing is old, huge, and heavy. Trystan glances at me from the corner of his eye. I waive the pillow at him. It nearly knocks me off balance. "I'm serious, Scott. We both have shitty lives. Mine is covered in glitz so people don't bother to notice, but I'm not stupid. And I'm not letting you give in to it. Get up."

When Trystan doesn't move, I swing the pillow at him. I try to do it gently, but there is no gently with these things. It's too big. The pillow hits him in the side of the face and makes a smacking sound. Trystan actually sways sideways. He glances at me with a shocked look on his face. The corners of my lips curl up. "You know you liked it." I waggle my eyebrows at him and he laughs.

Trystan stands and plucks a pillow from the couch, but not before I have the chance to whack him again. The pillow is too heavy. It pulls me forward every time I swing. When it smacks Trystan, it sounds like I hit him with a ream of paper. He rounds on me with that boyish grin on his face, and then nearly falls over. I laugh, but

Trystan already has his footing back. He taps me lightly with his pillow, like I might break.

"What the hell was that, Scott?" I tease him and bounce on the balls of my feet. I taunt him and say, "Play like you mean it."

"You like it rough?" The corner of his mouth twitches.

"No holding back. Not now. Not ever." I say the words and know that I'm not talking about a pillow fight. I'm talking about us, about what's happening between us and to us. I don't want to give up and I don't want to lose him.

I swipe my pillow at his arm. It took a mega-swing to get momentum, but I manage. When the pillow collides with Trystan, he staggers to the side before dropping his pillow. His blue eyes are crystal clear. Trystan steps toward me, pulls the pillow from my hands, and slides his palms up my cheeks and then tangles his fingers in my hair.

A rush of tingles shoots through my middle. I can't breathe. Trystan looks at me like I'm air and that he can't breathe without me. He brings our faces closer, so slowly that it feels like I'm going to die, but then our lips touch and everything changes. Butterflies fill my stomach. They swoop inside of me, making me giddy. The spots on my face where his palms touch my skin are electrified. A current shoots through me and makes me tingle.

And his lips, oh God, his lips—they press lightly at first. His mouth is so soft, his lips are so full. It's like that kiss when we were rehearsing, and then suddenly it's not. Trystan stops holding back. His desperation hits me hard. The tension in his arms flows into his hands and onto my cheeks as he tightens his grip.

The heat from his body encompasses me and I'm lost, falling through space. My eyes close and little white spots flicker behind my eyes. His hands slip over my skin and carefully move down my back and under my shirt. I gasp and press my mouth harder to his. The kiss is urgent, demanding. It's like we both know our time together is limited and everything is going to change. I can't stop and I don't want to. Heat seers under my skin as Trystan's hands slip over me. His tongue licks the seam of my lips, teasing me. My heart beats harder, and drowns out every other sound. When I open my mouth and let him, I feel my body going limp in his arms.

Trystan holds me to his chest and kisses me harder, deeper. His tongue moves in my mouth and I'm floating and falling at the same time. I don't come up for air. I'm afraid he'll stop. I'm afraid of what will happen next. I'm afraid…

Trystan barely breathes as the kiss endures. It's seeking, giving, and hoping. It's everything that I though a kiss should be, but he pulls away too soon. Trystan's face is flushed. Heat fills his cheeks and he breathes like he's run too far, too fast. His fingers brush my cheek and rest on my shoulder. "I love you, Mari." His sapphire gaze locks with mine. We hold each other. We say nothing.

The moment remains perfect, as if it's suspended in time. We cling to each other, hoping to God that there's more for us, that there's a way I can hold onto him. But, Trystan is like a snowflake. I'm afraid that if I try to close my hand around him, he'll disappear from my life. Trystan can't accept who he is, that it stems from where he came from. He won't forgive himself for this. Somehow I know it, but I can't let it go. I can't let him go. I love him with every ounce of my being, and I know that I always will.

CHAPTER 6

~TRYSTAN~

Mari is amazing. It doesn't matter what's wrong, she brings Trystan back to life.

He moves through the school and goes to his classes like it's any other day. Trystan smiles and jokes, but it's different now. That hollow feeling inside his chest has someone to fill it. Mari knows him like no one else. She understands him. Trystan wishes so badly that Mari didn't, but at the same time, he's glad she does. It's one of those things that he can't explain.

And right now he feels caught. Trystan can go on without her, but he doesn't want to. Love isn't like that, is it? Is it selfish? He didn't think so, and keeping Mari in his life is selfish. Things will only get worse. Trystan is falling down a pit, head first. He knows he's mid free-fall, and that he took Mari with him. The crap with his father isn't over. Add to the fact that he's homeless and his life is just getting worse.

But… but if he leaves Mari alone, her father will crush her. The light in her eyes will disappear. She'll give in and be what he wants, which is that demur version of Mari. Trystan brings out the other side of her, the real Mari. The one that is all vibrant and fantastic. The side she hides from the world.

Trystan glances across the stage. Mari is in the wing. The stage lights cast a golden glow on her skin as she waits for her cue. Her long hair is soft and totally touchable. When Mari woke him this morning, Trystan thought he was dreaming. Any touch from her sends him reeling. It's like she's his angel, his second chance, but somehow that isn't what's happened. Instead of pulling him up, he's sucking her down. Trystan swallows hard. The thoughts pummel his mind in a relentless wave. He'd give anything for her—do anything to make her happy. After last night—

His thoughts are cut off when Mari senses his gaze and looks up at him. She smiles. That soft, shy smile drives him crazy. He winks at her, knowing that it'll conceal his thoughts. Mari has a way of reading him that scares him to death. One glance at his eyes and she knows exactly what he's thinking. Hiding things from her is difficult.

Trystan honed in on things that set her off balance a while ago and uses them judiciously to set her off kilter when she gets too close. Damn it. He really needs to make up his mind and pull her in or push her away. *You don't deserve her*, a small voice reminds him. It's the same voice that said *don't fight back*. Trystan doesn't know what that is anymore. Last night, when the voice said to be still, he nearly died because of it. Maybe he's been listening to the wrong voice all this time? Maybe he should have fought back before now. He doesn't know and dwelling on it won't change anything.

Trystan takes his cue and enters the stage, while banishing the whole mess from his mind. He says his lines perfectly and it's all Mari's doing. When he enters the stage to act opposite her, Trystan can't help beaming. His smile is at full wattage. The acting is a reprieve, a chance to pretend that his horrid life doesn't exist. It's a chance to escape, and escaping it with Mari makes his time on stage even better.

They act—they fight, they banter, they kiss—it's as if this is a dream. If only life were this simple.

If only saying a few well-chosen words could really fix his mistakes. Trystan grins and pulls Mari close. She has that shy thing going on. It drives him crazy. The stage lights make her more radiant than she already is. Trystan can't think about anything but kissing her when her eyes lower like that, and she looks up at him from under her lashes.

Mari says her lines, but it feels real. For half a second, Trystan is lost in the scene. He's not himself. His past is gone, his pain is gone. Mari holds his heart and there is nothing else. They're in their own world and there is nothing weighing them down, no one to hold them back or break them apart. Mari looks at his eyes and he's lost in her gaze. There's no place better than this. It feels real. It feels like this could be his life, like he could have Mari and make her happy. For a second, hope floats into his chest and it feels so real that he can taste it. Then, the lights fade into blackness. The moment fractures as the curtain swings halfway closed and abruptly stops.

Mari is breathing hard. She steps away from him. Their relationship is still a secret. She glances at him out of the corner of her eye and smirks before exiting the stage. Trystan watches her walk around to the back of the theater and out the door. His eyes trail her slender frame too long.

Seth is sitting in the empty auditorium with a few other people. They mill around while we try to run through the entire play from start to finish, with lighting, and sound. The mic guy is doing well. There are hardly any issues with him, but the lighting guy is having problems with the spots.

Working with the lights on is awesome, but they're really warm. Trystan is glad they shut them off when he walks toward the front of the stage. He lowers himself and swings his legs off the edge and sits, looking out at vacant chairs. Trystan pushes his hair out of his eyes. Tucker and the lighting crew are yelling back and forth. The guy in the lighting cage curses and the lights dim.

Then, the remaining stage lights turn off completely. Tucker is yelling at them to switch to the spot, but they turn on a set of lights behind him. Trystan looks back behind him at the golden light, blocking his eyes with his arm, wondering how many more times they'll need to run through it tonight before everyone leaves.

Trystan wonders how long he can hide out in the basement without going home, how long it will be until he's caught.

CHAPTER 7

~MARI~

I love this. It's a rush, so much more than I thought it would be. Standing on stage, feeling the lights on my skin. There's no way to describe it. Add to the fact that I'm Trystan's co-star and it feels like a dream. Everything about him is contagious. He's dazzling on stage. He connects with me, calls to me, like we're two ends of the same string. I feel him tugging by just listening to his voice. It's magic and it's all Trystan.

I want to run and throw my arms around his neck when we take a break. I want to have that comfortable feeling of being close to him, but I can't. It's easier this way, I keep telling myself. Katie will have a stroke and I really don't need more crap from Seth or Brie right now. It's better that no one knows.

I smirk at Trystan. He returns the look with his blue eyes sparkling, before I run down the staircase on the side of the stage and up an aisle. I need a drink. I don't know how Trystan does it, especially since I know his throat is still sore from last night, but he's talking like nothing ever happened. It makes me wonder how many times he came in to school broken and battered and I didn't notice.

That smile of his hides so much pain.

Blinking hard, I push through the doors and smack into Brie. She's instantly irritated. "Watch where you're going, heifer." Brie shakes her head and her golden hair settles onto her shoulders before she shoves past me and into the auditorium.

I glance after her, wondering what she's doing here. I decide not to overreact. She's not a threat. Her part was given to me. It's not like Tucker will just hand it back. I turn and walk the few paces to the water fountain and drink. The water cools my throat.

When I walk back into the theater, I stand at the back half-wall, draping my arms on it. It's right when you walk in and separates the seats from the back aisle and the doors. Brie is a couple rows in front of me. She's slouched in a seat, but when they mess up the lights and blind everyone, Trystan turns around. For a moment, there's a halo of golden light around him. I smile. He looks like his video. My eyes drift to Brie. I wonder if she notices. If she does, she doesn't say anything.

A moment later Seth settles on the wall next to me. His voice is low, his lips barely moving, "What's the tramp doing here?"

"I don't know, but I don't like it. She's messed with Trystan enough to last a lifetime. I wish she'd fall down a hole or something."

Seth turns his face toward me and lifts a brow. "Is that venom from Little Goodie Two Shoes? I'm impressed."

"It's not unjustified." I watch Trystan dangling his legs off the side of the stage. I watch Brie watching him. It makes me nervous. He has enough pain in his life. He doesn't need anything else to go wrong. "She's got Trystan in her crosshairs."

He nods and looks back at his friend. Seth's expression softens and he sighs. "You care about him?"

"I'm not going to dignify that with a response," I say, tightly.

"I'm just saying, if you do—help me keep an eye on that one. I got his back for most of the day, but when he's in here…"

I glance at Seth. He's staring at Trystan unblinking. I wonder if he knows. Instead of asking, I lower my gaze and nod. "Done." Before Seth can say anything else and ruin my new, higher opinion of him, I walk back toward the stage.

Brie stands at the same time and smiles at me. It's one of those smiles that's good and pure, but when it's coming from someone like her, you know it's an evil omen. I narrow my eyes into slits as I pass her. She's trying to spook me. What could Brie possibly do to make life worse?

Tucker claps his large hands and thunder booms through the empty room. "Back on stage. Let's repeat the end of that last scene so the lighting guys can get their glitch fixed. Come on! Let's go!" He waives his arm toward the stage in a sweeping motion.

I climb the stairs and go back to the wing opposite Trystan. My stomach does a free fall when I see him. In the shadows, across the stage, Trystan looks up at me through his dark hair. He winks and I feel the need to giggle hysterically. I hear my cue and walk on stage. We run the scene two more times until lights and sound are at one hundred percent.

Tucker is pleased. Instead of pinching his nose, he's smiling at us. He stands at the edge of the stage. "You guys should be proud. You worked hard and it's obvious. Mari, thank you for stepping in at the last second. You are a perfect fit for this part. I hope to see you in more productions next year." I nod and smile awkwardly. Everyone looks at me. Trystan is standing next to me and bumps my shoulder with his. It attracts Tucker's attention. "And you, Scott. Try to refrain from doing anything stupid. We need you here, in one piece, tomorrow night." He rubs his palms together. "All right! Get out of here. See everyone back tomorrow night at 5:00pm. Don't be late!"

Trystan and I walk away from each other. I glance at him over my shoulder briefly. He's laughing, talking to Sophie about something. God, could she flirt with him more? Just as I'm thinking it, Trystan turns back and grins at me. I smile, and roll my eyes.

After I collect my stuff from backstage, I realize that I forgot a book and head back to my locker. The hallways are empty and the lights are off. I'm not supposed to be wandering the halls. I stop in front of my locker and rest my head on the metal, wondering how to help Trystan. I wish I could snap my fingers and make everything better for both of us.

"Are you holding up the wall with that pretty head of yours?" Trystan says softly. I turn my face and glance down the hall. He's standing with his hands in his pockets a few lockers down.

I sigh and straighten. "Someone has to."

He walks towards me, and his smile slips off his lips. Trystan is serious and that makes me more nervous than anything else. "Thank you. For not saying anything about last night. I know you're hurt." He's actually talking about it. When I tried to ask him this morning, he wasn't ready. But he is now.

"I know you're hurt. I wish I knew. I wish you'd told me." I can't look at him. Guilt is swallowing me whole. I'm the crappiest friend alive. I had no idea, none at all.

"There was nothing you could have done. Mari, this shit is normal. The cops don't even come anymore. I'm lucky they didn't toss me in jail last night. I'm eighteen. That arrest would have been permanent. I got lucky this time. There can't be a next time." He's next to me. His voice is soft, his breath is in my ear.

I know he wants me to turn to look at him, but I can't. Something is strangling me from the inside. I want to fix this. I know I can help him, at least a little bit. I know he can't go home anymore. I know he has no clothes. These are things I can offer. Before I even realize what I'm saying, the words are out of my mouth. "Then, stay with me. Hide out at my house until you graduate." I glance at him from the corner of my eye. My heart is beating too hard, too fast.

He laughs. "Your dad hates me—"

"My dad's never home. Last night after everything that happened, he didn't even call to see if I was all right. He stayed and worked his entire shift. The only thing he cares about is work and my mother." Trystan's eyes search my face. I turn toward him and press my back into the lockers. A sad smile lines my lips. Glancing at his chest, I say, "I shouldn't complain. Compared to you—"

He shakes his head. Dark hair falls in his eyes. Trystan's hands land on my shoulders. "Don't say that. Compared to me, you have your own hell. Compared to me, you're in just as much pain. I see it, Mari. It's written on your face and chiseled into your heart."

Trystan's eyes lower for a moment. His hand slips across my cheek, leaving a warm trail on my cool skin. "I wish I could take it away," he breathes. "I wish they'd see how wonderful and special and amazing you are. I don't know how your parents *can't* see that. They must be blind.

"You outshine the sun, Mari. And I'm not just saying that. It's true. When I look at you..." he breathes hard and rests his head against mine. "I see everything I ever wanted and more." By the time he finishes, his voice is a whisper.

I don't look at his eyes. I'll fall apart. Moving slowly, Trystan brushes his lips across my cheek. Every part of me reacts to his touch, to him. I'm breathing too hard. It's too hot. Trystan pulls back. There's a breath between us and no more. My heart hammers inside of me. We're like two magnets, slightly separated, pulling toward each other. When I lift my gaze to meet his, I melt. My lips part and I breathe. Trystan lowers his lashes and watches my mouth. I'm falling. I'm lost in his gaze.

Trystan is about to kiss me when a jarring voice slams through the hall.

"Oh, no. Not this shit again. Scott, you said you were over this." Seth walks toward us. His boots echo up and down the hall. He's as graceful as a gorilla with concrete sneakers.

Trystan gives me a look that says he's sorry and a million other things. Before Seth gets closer, he leans in and whispers in my ear, "I'll come. After seven?" I nod. Trystan's eyes meet mine and the only thing I want is his arms around me.

He winks at me and turns away. Trystan is all swagger and charm.

He struts away saying, "You know how much I like to tease her." He looks over his shoulder at me. I play back and give him a pointed expression. Trystan laughs and grabs Seth's shoulders, pulling him away from me. "Come on. Let's grab dinner. I'm starving."

Seth looks at Trystan and then back at me, saying, "We had an understanding Jennings and this isn't part of it." Seth gives me a hostile look and points his finger at me. "You're back on my shit list."

"I was never off your shit list," I huff and slam my locker door. I walk down the hall and shove past them, adding, "And I don't really care if I'm on your list or not, Seth. Have fun making out with yourself, Sexbot." I feel their eyes on me.

My heart is flying, soaring so high, so fast. Trystan said yes. He'll stay over. Nothing could ruin this night. Nothing.

CHAPTER 8

~TRYSTAN~

Seth doesn't drop it. As soon as Mari disappears from sight he hisses, "I thought you were over her?"

Trystan keeps that distant look in his eye. He never tells Seth much of anything. The guy panics. He wants Trystan's life to make sense to him, but it doesn't. Hell, it doesn't even make sense to Trystan. How is he supposed to explain anything to the guy?

"Maybe I'm just friends with her," Trystan says, "and maybe I don't want to rehash this whole thing with you tonight. Do me a favor, okay? If you still can't stand her on Monday, tell me and we can discuss it then." Trystan says, pushing his hair out of his eyes. "From the way your acting, it seems like you liked Brie better."

Seth's eyes get a little too big for his head. "You're into her, too? Damn man." He grins. "You think you can get 'em both at once?"

Trystan's fingers flinch. Instead of slugging his friend, he smiles and nods. Trystan says things he doesn't mean, wishing for things he doesn't want. Mari and Brie. As if that was something to hope for. Trystan shakes off the skeeved layer sticking to his skin and changes the subject. "I heard you were talking about enlisting?"

Trystan couldn't believe it. When they were in lab, he heard a teacher mentioning Seth's lack of teacher recommendation forms. The teacher from across the hall said Seth was enlisting. It was weird to find out that way.

Seth doesn't look a Trystan. Instead, he nods and says, "Yeah, I mean, it's not like I'm a nerd and can get into a good college. Besides, I haven't got cash for that kind of shit."

"I know what you mean." Trystan and Seth weave their way through the school as they talk, and then exit the front of the building.

The air is crisp, like it might snow. There are about two hours until he has to be at Mari's house. Two hours to kill with Seth. He breathes in deeply and runs his fingers through his hair. "I was going to enlist, but I don't know anymore…"

Seth gives him a look. "Dude, you're seriously going to let me enlist by myself? Why do you think I went to the recruiter?"

Trystan gives his friend an awkward smile, "Thanks, but there is no way you should enlist to hang out with me. I'm headed nowhere too fast."

Seth laughs, "Well, it's better to have company along the way. I mean, who else is going to be your wing man when they send you to China or some shit?"

"I don't think we have troops in China." Trystan glances at Seth and tries not to smile. The guy is about to sign on the dotted line and has no idea about anything, which sounds about right for Seth. "Besides, I might not enlist anyway. I've been thinking about doing something else."

"Like…?" Seth asks, knowing as well as Trystan does that there aren't many options. Neither of them is exceptionally anything.

Trystan shrugs. "The hell if I know. I'm just saying, don't enlist because of me. There's a chance I'm not going to do it."

Seth is staring at a car full of girls in track uniforms. Seth and the girls are hollering at each other. The man isn't even listening anymore. The girls pull over to the side of the road. "Hey hotties! Want a ride?" One girl asks and they all start giggling. Seth's eyes go wide, like he's being called to the mother-ship.

Trystan grabs Seth's arm and waves them off, "Not tonight, ladies." The car full of girls takes off, leaving behind streamers of white smoke and giggles.

"What the hell was that for? What'd I ever do to you?" Seth whines.

"I want to eat dinner. Plus I gotta be somewhere in an hour, so get your ass moving or I'll have to eat without you." Trystan starts walking again. Seth waits a beat, and then follows. Trystan has eight bucks in his pocket. It's the last of his money from Sam. He'll have to go bust his ass after school next week and earn more.

"You have something set up?" Seth asks, his voice filled with innuendo.

Trystan shoves his hands in his pockets and stares straight ahead, wishing the diner would materialize and suck them through the front doors so he wouldn't have to take part in this conversation. "Something."

"Way to be vague, Scott. Come on, man, who's the lucky girl? You think she'll put out?"

Trystan smirks and laughs. That's the last thing that he expects to happen. The night will probably be filled with Mari's voice and lips, and maybe if he's lucky, her dad won't come home early and beat the shit out of him. Repeating last night is the last thing he wants to do. But still, it's worth the risk. Deciding to go to Mari's is one of the stupider things he's done.

"Come on, Trystan. Give names, man. Who are you gonna nail?" Seth yips like a dog, begging for scraps. He's relentless and doesn't stop until they walk into the diner. He scans the booths for girls they know. "Nicole's over there." Seth says, hopeful.

"So go sit with her if you want. I'll be over here." Trystan points, and follows the waitress. Seth seems to be stuck. You could see the guy getting pulled in two directions.

Seth finally follows Trystan to the booth and sits down. He grabs a menu and then something weird happens.

The girl sitting across from them says, "If it's not my two favorite idiots." Katie sweeps her long hair over her shoulder, tosses a tip on the table and walks over. "How's it hanging, Trystan?" She places her fingers on their table and cocks her head to the side. "Cuz if you mess with my girl Mari, I'm gonna make you wish—"

"Mari's at home, and I didn't do anything to her." Trystan says, tightly. He wonders what Katie knows, if anything. She's Mari's best friend. They're always together.

Seth is watching Katie a little too closely. "Hey kitten, you want me to make you purr?" Seth grins at her and sweeps his eyes over her body, lingering way too long on her breasts.

Katie's mouth falls open. When she snaps back to life, Katie swings her purse and pegs Seth in the side of the head. He makes a noise like a pig bouncing out of the back of a pickup truck, and then clutches his head between his hands. "What. The. Fuck." He glares at Katie.

Katie's pissed. Her jaw is locked and when she talks, she sounds like she'll rip his face off. "Don't talk to me, Seth. So help me God—"

Katie is interrupted by the waiter. "Is there a problem over here?" the waiter asks, looking at each of them in turn.

Trystan beams and shakes his head. "Nope. We're ready to order though." He goes ahead, ordering three plates of food, fries, and shakes. When the waiter leaves, Trystan points at Katie and then the booth. "Sit down, Katie Scarlett," he says with a thick Irish brogue.

She lifts a dark brow at him. The girl could eat them alive. She'd spit out their bones and ask for seconds. There's a fierce thing going on with her, that's for certain. "You think I'm that vapid skank from Gone with the Wind? Seriously?"

"No," Trystan replies with a smirk on his face. "I just thought you liked big hats. Besides, that's the only famous Katie I know."

Seth offers, "Katie Couric."

Trystan inclines his head toward Katie. They lock gazes. Katie's expression is telling Trystan to piss off, but that look tells him that he's right. She'd happily slaughter them both with her purse. Seth got off easy. God help the poor bastard who dates this girl. "Katie Couric doesn't have the same spunk as Katie Scarlett."

"Who the fuck is Katie Scarlett?" Seth blurts out way too loud. That pretty much sums up dinner. Seth and Katie bicker for an hour and Trystan tries to derail everything by throwing them off their game. It works, but not for long. It's as though they like fighting with each other. Eventually, he just sits back and watches and develops a deep respect for Katie in the process.

CHAPTER 9

~MARI~

When I get home, I'm blindsided. I walk through the door and drop my book bag on the floor. I expect to be alone. My parents go out to dinner together on Thursday nights, but tonight they didn't go. Tonight they're home, waiting for me.

"Mari dear, pick up your school bag and put it away." Mom's voice meets me before I find her in the kitchen. I don't double back for my books.

"What's wrong? Why are you still here?" I glance around, looking for Daddy, but I don't see him.

Mother replies, "There was an important development with the lawsuit. That girl you punched in the face came by looking for you. Your father sent her away, but her parents called later." She moves through the kitchen getting a lunch bag ready. She puts in a sandwich and pours the coffee into a travel mug. She glances at me. "We worked everything out. If you apologize, they'll drop the suit."

"What?" I squeak. My hackles rise. I can't stand it. I can't believe she even said it. "You want me to apologize to her? You realize that this is the same person who bullied me every day for the past three years? This is the same person who—"

Mother gives me a look that makes me stop talking. It doesn't matter what I say. The decision was made without me. I press my eyes closed and sigh way too loud. I want to scream at her. I want her to act like she loves me and not like a goddamn robot all the time. She tries so hard to make my dad happy, like he's the only thing that matters. Why'd they even have me? I don't understand. I doubt I ever will.

Mother's voice carries a warning when she speaks. "Go upstairs and apologize. She's been waiting for you."

My eyes go so wide that they nearly fall out of my head and roll across the floor. "What? What did you say?"

"She's in your room, Mari. You've kept her waiting long enough already. Go apologize and you better be nice. If this blows up, your father won't like it." She glares at me and wipes down the counter. I stare at her. It's the only thing I can do. Screaming at Mother doesn't help. It's like she's a hollowed out shell. It doesn't matter how loudly I speak, she won't hear me. Mom would let me sign away my own life if it made my dad happy.

Gritting my teeth, I say, "Fine." I sprint-walk toward my room and fly up the stairs. When I pull the door open, Brie is standing in front of my desk. She was obviously looking through things.

"Hey, virgin," she beams and waves the tips of her fingers at me. "My daddy said you owe me an apology. So let's have it." She folds her narrow arms over her ample chest and tilts her head to the side, obviously pleased.

I want to pull her hair out. I want Brie to go away and leave me alone. I knew she was gunning for me and this is lightweight for Brie. I suppose I should be happy, but I still want to shove her down a well. I manage a fake smile, and say in my nice voice, "I'm so sorry I hurt you, Brie."

There's something about the look in Brie's eye that tells me that she already got what she came here for. My stomach falls into my shoes when she walks past me, her heels clicking on the floor. Leaning closer, she whispers, "This isn't over, Mary. I don't need my daddy to fight my battles for me. Watch your back." She smiles at me like she couldn't be more pleased.

My heart pounds harder. My fingers ball into fists at my sides. I'm so close to snapping. I don't care if my dad gets sued. It'd be worth it. But something holds me back. I don't clothesline her and shove her down the stairs. Brie leaves my room. I don't follow her out. Instead, I sit down hard on my bed and hold my head between my hands. How could they? Betrayal snakes up my throat and tastes vile.

Mother's voice carries up to my room. The door is open. I hear her thank Brie for her kind, forgiving, spirit and wish her a good evening. Then, Mother walks up the stairs. I hear her familiar footfalls and I wish so badly that she tried to help me, just once. I need her. I want her, but she's never there.

"Now, that wasn't so hard was it?" She's standing in my doorway with her jacket on over her scrubs.

"How would you know? You aren't the one who stood up for yourself and then had to apologize to the asshat that was harassing you. Was that you? Because I thought that was me?"

"Don't be so dramatic, Mari. This will end well, and before it wouldn't have. Be thankful that she was so forgiving." Mom walks into the room, and fluffs a pillow on the bed next to me. She doesn't sit by me, she doesn't offer any support whatsoever.

Tears are in my eyes. I shake my head and look up at her. "Yes, I'll remember how forgiving she is next time she hurts me. I'll remember how my mother liked Brie better than me, and I'll thank Brie for kicking my ass and invite her to tea!" I lose it. I'm standing, screaming in her face. I can't help it.

Instead of fighting back, my mother rolls her eyes and turns to leave. "Honestly, Mari. You're almost an adult. Such juvenile behavior is unbecoming."

She glances over my outfit, over the cami with no flannel, and scrunches up her nose. "And you are not to dress like this again. You look like a streetwalker in that shirt. The boys will think you're giving it away and then what will you do? You can't punch every person who offends you, dear." She looks back at me and smiles, like one of those TV moms that always knows best—the one with an apron and a pie in her hand—the one who is there when her children come home—the one who is there when they cry. My mom thinks she is that mother, and that all my cries for help are silly attempts to get her attention. It makes me crazy.

"Good night, mother," I say through gritted teeth. Too many thoughts race through my head. They are things I should never say, things I should never feel.

Mom leaves and I close the door behind her. Turning I press my back against the door and slide down to the floor. My hair sticks to the tears that refuse to stay in my eyes and fall down my cheeks. I push my tangled mess back and slide my palms over my eyes. When I look up, my gaze lands on the wall with the bulletin board. I stare for a moment. Something's different, but I don't know what.

CHAPTER 10

~TYRSTAN~

Ditching Seth is easier said than done. The guy doesn't want to part ways until he knows where Trystan is going. He wants specifics. Trystan won't give any. Seth finally caves in and follows some girls out of the diner, which pisses Katie off to no end. She abruptly leaves and says a few choice words to Seth.

That breaks up their little party and Trystan is free of them.

It's dark and chilly out again, like it might snow, which is bad since Trystan is homeless. He takes his time walking along the streets, weaving his way past the pristine homes as he heads toward Mari's house. When he arrives, he sees a light in kitchen. A woman stands at the window. She's tall and slender with Mari's dark hair. *That must be her mother.* Trystan glances at his watch. It's past 7:00pm.

He waits and the woman finally shuts off the lights and leaves. When her car travels down the street, Trystan pulls out the cell that Mari gave him. He keeps walking, not wanting to linger in front of her house. He walks down to the end of the block and turns the corner, planning on coming up to the house from behind, like last time. He texts Mari:

Can I come up?

A few seconds pass and then:

Yes. I'll b down in a sec

Trystan turns at the corner and heads back in the direction of Mari's house. He cuts through the backyard directly behind her house and squeezes through the gap in the fences. Soon he's standing on her back patio. Mari is in the open door, looking down at him. Light spills around her, creating a perfect silhouette. She looks so beautiful. Everything about Mari is so far out of his reach, so why is he reaching? Does it matter if she loves him?

Our lives are so different.

But they're so similar, too. Wealth doesn't get rid of abusive parents. It just hides the damage better. Trystan feels a flutter in his chest, like he shouldn't be here—like something bad is going to happen. He remains on the patio and holds Mari's gaze for too long.

"Are you going to come in?" she says, smiling at him. Tension creases the spot in the center of her forehead like something's wrong. Trystan can't leave her alone. Not now. Not when she needs him. Any second thoughts about being at Mari's vanish.

Trystan grins at her, wanting to see her smile. He wants that worry line pressed flat, erased like it was never there. "Do you always invite boys into your room when your parents leave, Mari Jennings? I had you pegged for a good girl. To think, all this time, I was totally wrong." He teases her with each step he takes, closing the distance between them. When he's in front of the door, Mari still hasn't opened it. She stands on the other side of the screen in a cami and a pair of jeans. His eyes drift to the bare skin at her neck and arms, then back to her face. "You look beautiful tonight."

"Flattery will get you nowhere, Mr. Scott." Mari looks at him from under those dark lashes and smiles. Every inch of skin burns for her touch when she gives him that look.

"I'm not so sure about that. Let me in and let's find out." Trystan grins and she breaks his gaze. Looking away, Mari tucks a curl behind her ear and opens the door. Trystan brushes past her just as

Mari turns to the side. It aligns their chests so that they barely touch as he passes. The sensation shoots through him in a crippling wave that takes his breath away. Trystan sucks in air softly, trying to hide how much she rattles him.

Mari turns toward him. Those big dark eyes are filled with remorse. He can see it. He can read it on her face, in her stance, and the way she holds her fingers and twists each one. Trystan wants to ask what happened, but he doesn't want to invade her privacy. It's weird. There's a spot where he wants to be, and it is invasive. That spot is smack in the center of all her most intimate thoughts and feelings—the ones that no one else knows. Trystan doesn't speak. Instead, he steps toward her and pulls Mari to his chest. His hands find her hair and he just holds her gently. Mari's hands lift and slip under Trystan's jacket. She buries her face in his shoulder and stares blankly.

Mari looks up at him with that expression on her face, and Trystan feels like he's going to shatter into too many pieces. He kisses her forehead and whispers, "What's wrong?"

Mari's eyes fall to the floor. She doesn't let go of him. "My mom decided to humiliate me instead of paying a settlement to Brie's dad. It's nothing. I don't want to talk about it."

Trystan splays his fingers and runs them through her hair, forcing Mari to look up at him. A million emotions flash across her eyes. He doesn't press her. "Then, we won't."

Mari smiles softly. She steps away from him and walks away. Trystan remains frozen by the door, his eyes sweeping over her back and drinking in her curves. Mari glances back at him and extends her hand. "Come on. I have something in my room for you."

Trystan smirks and takes her hand, not bothering to contain his excitement. "That is quite a line, kiss ninja."

Mari laughs and bumps him with her shoulder. "I didn't mean it like that! You're so stupid, Scott. I swear—"

"Nah, you like me like this. Admit it." They walk up the staircase to her room side by side.

"You wouldn't want me if I were all polite and proper. For instance, telling you that I intend to kiss every inch of your bare skin later is something that I would say. Telling you that you're pretty isn't something that would ever fall out of my mouth. Mainly because it's such a ridiculous understatement that—"

Mari releases his hand and turns suddenly, pushing him into the wall. She leans into him and presses her body against his. Mari's pink lips linger so close, but she doesn't close the distance between them. The sudden action makes his heart lurch. Her hand presses into his chest and remains there with her fingers splayed. Her breath is warm and sweet. Trystan wants to taste her so badly, but Mari doesn't kiss him. Her eyes only sweep over his face, and then land on his lips.

When she speaks, he thinks he might die and tumble down the stairs. "I admit it. I like you this way. I expect you to say the unexpected, to do things to knock me off balance and make me drop my guard. I know you do it on purpose, but for the longest time I didn't know why. Now I do, and I think things are going to get very interesting between us. Don't you think?" She smiles the sexiest smile he's ever seen and traces the tips of her finger along his jaw, barely touching his skin.

Breathless, Trystan says, "You know me so well." He tries hard to hide it, but he can't. His body hums when she touches him. Those perfectly pink lips are so close.

When Mari spoke, they touched his mouth with a light brush. The sensation is still shooting through him. It makes him want more. "So, are you planning on having your way with me on the stairs?"

Mari's face flames red. She laughs. "You're such an ass." Mari releases him and walks up a step.

Trystan repeats her swift movement and pins her to the wall. His hips press into hers and she gasps. There's no question about what she does to him. His eyes meet hers. His heart pounds harder. He leans in and brushes his lips across hers so lightly. It's a ghost of a kiss, as subtle as a whisper. He pulls back and Mari gasps and grabs her heart. The smirk on Trystan's face says he's playing, toying with her, but he's not. He'd kiss her like that all night, if he could.

Mari's knees are shaky after that. She tries to push off the wall and stand, but one leg doesn't cooperate and she falls into him. Trystan holds her arm and grins. "Took your breath away, did I?"

"You're evil," she says, smiling, still breathless. "We seriously need to get you a long black cloak and a helmet."

"We could, but I think that'd just turn you on." Trystan laughs as they walk up the stairs together and reach the upper landing. He follows Mari into her room. On her bed are some towels and a pair of jeans and a shirt, folded and stacked into a neat pile.

The smile fades from Trystan's lips. "What's this?"

Mari walks over to the pile and thrusts it at Trystan before she turns to the little bathroom in her room. "I thought you'd want to shower and change." She's opening the bathroom door and flicks on the lights. "I can reapply the make up around your neck in the morning. I'm guessing the bruise is an awesome shade of green now. Mine is." She lifts the hem of her shirt. The bruise on her belly is purple with green tinges around the edges. She lifts her gaze and looks at him, still holding onto her shirt.

Trystan's mouth has gone dry. He steps toward her and sets the clothes and towels down on the counter before slipping his hand around her middle. "I'm so sorry for this. So sorry." His voice is soft, barely audible. Something creeps up his throat and chokes him.

Trystan's fingers trace the bruise slowly, gently. Mari takes a slow breath, but exhales jaggedly. When he looks up, he sees her eyes and realizes what his touch did. While he was mourning his previous actions, she was frozen by his touch. Mari closes her eyes and blinks slowly, like she's trying to snap out of it. But she can't. Not as long as he's touching her like this.

Trystan withdraws his touch and runs his hand through his hair. Mari's chest swells as she breathes in. It draws attention to her breasts. It makes him wonder what it would feel like to hold them in his hands. Trystan tears his gaze away. Although Mari said she changed her mind that one time, she hasn't mentioned sex again. Trystan already decided that he won't pressure her. He won't sleep with her no matter what happens tonight.

Trystan gathers his wits and picks up the clothes and towels. "Thank you for this. I won't be long." Trystan slips past her into the bathroom and closes the door. For a moment, all he does it stare at the knob. He wants her so badly. He can't stand it. Every thought that fills his head is more forbidden than the last. The way Mari pressed him into the wall before set him on fire. Trystan knows he needs to calm down and put some distance between them or they'll end up tangled in her sheets faster than he can blink.

Trystan turns on the shower, making it as cold as he can tolerate.

CHAPTER 11

~MARI~

My heart is racing too hard. I didn't think that I could feel more attracted to Trystan than I already did, but when he touched me like that—oh my God. It was like every inch of my body was burning. I couldn't stop staring at his hands, willing them to touch me. I still haven't moved. I'm leaning against the wall, and finally hear the shower turn on. I wonder what Trystan looks like in there with the water running over his body. I think about how much I'd like to run my hands over him. I don't even realize that's what I'm thinking. I just feel the palm of my hand grow hotter and more sensitive. I think about his bare skin and the water. I blink hard, trying to free the thoughts from my mind.

Scolding myself, I push off the wall. What's the matter with me? When did I become this hornball who only thinks about sex? I pad across the room and grab a pair of sweats from my dresser. I strip quickly with my back to the bathroom door in case Trystan walks out. The water is still running, but I'm too nervous to think.

I'm mad at myself for acting like this, for melting so fast. He barely touched me and I'm falling to pieces. I tug my sweatshirt over my head and pull on a pair of fuzzy socks. This is the least sexy outfit I own. The sweatshirt is way too big. It swims on me. I yank my hair into a ponytail and jump up on the bed and flick on the TV. I try to stop thinking about him, but I can't. I watch a show without really seeing it.

When the water turns off, my heart beats faster. I wish I were a sane person. I wish for a lot of things that I can't have. I decide that I'm not doing anything with him tonight. I want more time. Plus, the bruises on my stomach and the way it aches, I just would rather he saw me the way I usually am. I realize what I'm thinking and feel the heat burn across my cheeks.

Trystan pulls open the bathroom door. He's bare-chested, wearing the new jeans around his hips, with no shoes. His hair is so dark and still dripping. There's a towel in his hand. Trystan wraps it around his shoulders. He notices my blush and says, "I love it when you do that." He smiles at me, winks, and then runs the towel over his head.

"I hate it when I do that, which seems to be all the time. It's not becoming at all." I realize I sound like my mother and flinch.

But Trystan doesn't care. He steps toward me with that sexy smile he always wears. "It's sexy as hell." He tugs at the towel and adds, "I can't say the same for this, and unless I wear a towel all night, you're going to see bruises. The thing is…" he looks down for a second. When his blue eyes lift, he meets my gaze. "I don't want you to fuss about it all night. The past is the past. I can't fix it. I would, if I could." Trystan's breathing hard, his chest is rising and falling too quickly. It pains me to see him like this.

"You can leave the towel on, if you want. Or…" I smile. I have an idea. I jump off my bed and cross the room. My dresser drawer has exactly what I need. Without thinking twice about it, I grab a pair of scissors and slice through the bottom of my sweatshirt. Trystan looks at me like I'm crazy. He flinches, his hands lifting until he realizes what I'm doing. I cut off the front bottom half of the shirt. It reveals my rainbow bruises as if they were framed. The scrap of fabric falls to the floor. I put the sheers down and turn back to him. "Better?"

Trystan grins. It makes those beautiful eyes sparkle like the sea in the afternoon sun. "Is there any other circumstance where you'd cut your clothes off like that? No? Are you sure." He looks at the floor and then back up at my face. He finally answers, "Yes, it's better."

I nod toward his towel. "Good, then drop it."

Trystan glances at me from the corner of his eye. He pulls the towel away. The angry marks around his neck look worse than last night. I try not to react. I lift my eyes to his. I step across the room and slip my arms around his waist. Trystan's eyes lock on mine, but there's something there, like he has to protect himself from me.

My fingers trace the warm, smooth skin at his waist. I say softly, "We're the same. You know that, right?"

Trystan's gaze remains locked with mine. He inhales sharply as my fingers move around to his back. There's a small space between us, both physical and mental. "Mari, don't..." It's all he can manage. His jaw is tight, locked shut. The muscles in his neck are corded like he can barely swallow.

I want him to relax, to feel safe for once. My godforsaken parents won't show up until dawn. There's no one to hurt him here. I have a sinking feeling in my stomach. Maybe he thinks that I'll hurt him. My eyes lower. My gaze traces the curves of the muscles on his chest, but I'm not brave enough to lift my hand. My heart beats harder. I want him to understand. I feel the pull to him, like we're two sides of the same coin. The fact that I'm shiny and he's not doesn't matter. We're connected. We're the same.

I don't look into his eyes again. I know what I want to do. Tugging his arm, I pull him toward my bed. I flick out the lights as I pass them. We're encased in darkness. Trystan doesn't move easily. It's like he's holding back. I finally say, "I just want to hold you. I want to sleep with your arms around me. No sex."

Trystan's voice catches when he speaks, "Mari, I don't know. I don't want to do anything you'll regret—"

"I won't regret this. I'll never regret this." I slip back on my bed, but he won't sit. His eyes pierce through me like a sword.

"You said this was something that was reserved for marriage." He's still looking at me. I smile softly. It turns out that all those times I scolded him for taking sex so lightly, he was listening. I almost wish he wasn't. He runs his hands through his hair and looks at me. "I don't think this is a good idea. I don't want you to resent me. These aren't whims with you. It's part of who you are. I can't do this to you."

I'm kneeling on the bed, looking at him. My eyes sweep over his face. He means well. Trystan wants to protect me. I understand, and I know he won't change his mind. "You're too good for me."

He laughs. It sounds so haunted and bitter that it kills me. "I doubt it. I heard I'm made of snails and puppy dog tails." Trystan grins at me and winks, quickly covering the emotions that played across his face seconds ago.

I lay back in my bed and he pulls up my blankets and tucks me in. Then, he settles on my floor at the foot of my bed. The clock ticks off the minutes, but I can't sleep. My eyes are wide open. After what feels like forever, I say, "Trystan?"

"Mmm?"

My throat is tight. "How do you manage everything? I mean, no one has any idea and you never give the slightest indication that anything is wrong.

"Some days I feel like I'm going to fall apart. You never seem weak like that. How do you do it? How do you brush off the fact that the people who are supposed to love you the most, don't love you at all?" My lip is quivering. Although I've thought it, I never had the guts to say it before. "I know they don't love me. I know they resent me, but I still can't accept it. I keep hoping that one day they'll really see me and love me for who I am, but that day never comes."

By the time I finish talking, I'm whispering. I don't want to admit the words to anyone, but I do. As I speak, the words crush me. The bitter truth is that I feel guilty that my parents don't love me. I feel like it's my fault. For a long time, I thought that if I was better or smarter—I thought that I could earn their love—but it didn't happen. Nothing changed. I stare at my ceiling without blinking. Thoughts stream from my head like rainwater down a gutter.

Trystan sits up. He's at the foot of my bed on the floor, looking up at me. His hair dried into that messy look he always wears. Pulling his knees into his chest, Trystan leans back against the side of my bed. "I think that's the key—admitting that the day will never come. It's the hardest part it. Hope just rips your heart apart with shit like this.

"There is no hope. There is no peace. Accepting it makes it easier to wade through the day to day stuff. But, I've done a crappy job at hiding it lately. My old man locked me in my room the other day after tossing all my things. He does stuff like that from time to time. It's supposed to remind me of my place. He says that over and over again, like it's a lesson that I need to learn. I know my fucking place."

Trystan takes a deep breath and runs both hands over the back of his neck, stretching as he does it. "Tucker figured it out. For the past few weeks he's been hinting, telling me it's okay to talk to him, but they don't get it. Dragging it out for everyone to see will just make it worse.

And I've got no right, but it makes me mad. Where was Tucker ten years ago? Where was he five years ago? It would have made a difference then. It won't do a goddamn thing now." Trystan startles and looks over his shoulder. His eyes meet mine. He smiles, sheepishly. "I didn't mean to say all that."

I shrug. "It needed to be said."

"How do you do that?" He stands and sits on the end of my bed.

"Do what?"

"How do you make me feel like this? I can be talking about the most horrible thing that ever happened to me, but with you here, the pain lessens. I feel like I'll get through it and everything might be all right after all."

I smile at him. I don't know what else to do. I'm lying back on my pillow. I cross my ankles under the blankets and tuck my hands behind my head. "'That's what you do for me. Maybe it's magic. Maybe you're my yang."

"Yang?" He gives me a weird look.

"Yeah, like on a yin yang. We reflect each other, despite everything." I watch him for a moment. His eyes are on mine. I pat the bed next to me and Trystan finally gives in. He crawls toward me and lays his head on my pillow. I turn on my side to look at him.

Trystan kisses my lips lightly and sighs. A smile pulls at the corners of his mouth. "Good night, beautiful girl."

CHAPTER 12

~TRYSTAN~

A car door slams and jerks Trystan awake. Early morning sunlight pours through Mari's windows. Trystan sits up and looks down at Mari, still asleep. That noise woke him up, made him jump. Call it conditioning from his father, but if Trystan didn't jump up and grab his things that second, he would be thrown out the window.

Trystan peeks out the bedroom door and sees Mari's dad. He's still wearing scrubs and is setting his things down on table in the hallway below. Panicked, Trystan doesn't know what to do. He can't sneak out. Her dad is blocking the way.

Trystan goes back to Mari and wakes her gently, kissing her cheek. She smiles and stretches. "Trystan." The way she says his name makes him reel, but he can't afford to think like that. Not now. If Mari's dad catches him, he's dead.

Whispering next her ear, he says, "Your dad is downstairs. I need to hide."

Before Trystan has a chance to say anything else, the sound of footfalls reaches their ears. Mari sits straight up in bed, her brown eyes wide like dinner plates. She points to the closet. Trystan takes his things and ducks inside and closes the door just before Mari's dad enters the room.

He bangs on the door and shouts, "Wake up, Mari. You're going to be late." He flicks on the lights and it fills the crack under the closet door. Trystan can hear him enter the room. His heart beats harder, faster. He pulls on his shoes and shirt without making a sound. Trystan feels like a coward hiding. He should run out and stand up to the man, but he can't. He can't even take care of himself. And getting found out won't help either of them.

"Mother said you apologized to Brie last night. I was glad to hear it.

No more of this, Mari. Now get dressed for school. And mind your mother. She said no more tight clothes. Do as she asks. I don't want to hear about my daughter looking like a street-walker ever again." The door clicks shut and he's gone.

Trystan cracks the closet door open and looks at Mari. The life has been sucked out of her. Her shoulders are slumped and her skin is sallow. The color in her cheeks is gone. There's no light in her eyes. He knows that look and wishes to God that he could take it away, but he can't. Even if they were older, Trystan doesn't have the money to save her from that man. Her dad crushed her just now and there was nothing he could do about it.

Mari glances up at him. She blinks slowly and smiles, but it doesn't reach her eyes. "You better go before Mom comes home and decides to go through my closet. You can climb down the trellis like you wanted to the other day. Dad is headed for the shower. Wait a second for the water to turn on and then go. I'll meet you in the basement at the school and fix up your neck."

Trystan doesn't know why he does it, but he does. He can't stand that flat listless voice. He can't bear to watch Mari like this. He crosses to her bed and pushes her back into her pillows while pressing his lips to hers. They both have morning breath, but he doesn't care. Trystan loves her. He wants her to be happy. He wants that smile on her face again. Trystan tangles his hands in her hair and lays on top of her, kissing her so hard that he can't breathe.

When he pulls back, she's smiling shyly. It's a perfectly Mari smile. "I love you," he whispers and bounces off her bed and heads to the window. Mari touches her fingers to her lips like she's dreaming.

Trystan sneaks out before anything else can go wrong.

CHAPTER 13

~MARI~

When I'm done pulling on my jeans and tee shirt, I bend over to find my boots. I kicked them under my desk the other night. When I pull them out, I see a piece of paper caught between the desk and the wall. I reach for it, instantly knowing what it is—Trystan's song. How'd it get on the floor? I go to pin it back in place, but decide that it shouldn't be where anyone could get it. If my parents took the song or Brie managed to get her hands on it, that'd be bad. So I take it with me, stuffing it into my jeans pocket.

I get to school early and head to find Trystan. The halls are empty. I pull open the basement door and run down the stairs. After that kiss this morning, I have a kiss of my own to give him. But when I reach the bottom of the landing, I freeze. He's singing softly. His back is turned to me, like he doesn't know I'm there. After a moment, he glances back at me and startles.

"Hey, ninja. Fancy meeting you here." Trystan's eyes sweep over me in a way that makes me feel beautiful.

"I heard there was a rock star living in the school basement. I had to see it for myself." I smile at him and drop my bag on the couch. Walking over to him slowly, I swing my leg over his lap and sit. We nearly fall off the little stool. He laughs and holds onto me with the guitar between us. "This was more romantic in my head."

He grins. Hard. "Kiss me, Mari."

The way he says it makes my heart jump. My stomach twists and that empty space inside my chest fills with warmth. I'm beaming at him, moving in slowly, crushing the guitar between us. My lips brush against his and then he's kissing me back. Trystan's hands find my face and he holds onto me, encouraging me, wanting me. My heart pounds harder and harder. I wish there was nothing but this moment now. I can understand this. I can deal with this. Everything else can fade away and I'd be happy. When we come up for air, I slip off his lap.

Trystan moans and puts the guitar back. "I wasn't done with you."

I'm still flushed. My lips are too sensitive. I can still feel his lips on my mouth. I smile and shake my head. I know how much it will devastate him if anyone saw the marks on his neck. "You need make-up first. Kisses later."

He gives me a funny look. "I never thought I'd hear that sentence."

I laugh. He tugs a loop on the waistband of my jeans and pulls me close. His hands lace through my hair and he kisses me again. I don't want to pull away. I moan and say, "We're running out of time."

He sighs and gives me a serious look. "What if we just said you gave me some really wicked hickeys?" That makes me laugh even louder. The smile that stretches across his face when I laugh is beautiful. It's Trystan without anything hindering him or weighing him down.

I shove him back down to the stool. "Sit. Let me do this before the bell rings."

"Fine, but you're going to have to talk about something else. A guy only has so much self-control, and your chest is right in front of my face. Honestly, I'm having a lot of trouble not jumping on you and covering you in kisses." He smirks, his eyes still way below my neckline.

The way he says it is so casual, like he might actually do it. Part of me wants him to. My pulse is racing, making it so I only hear the steady, swift, beating and my breaths. I reach toward him and take his chin in my hand and tilt it up to my face. His blue gaze is dazzling. It's like someone's lit a flame inside of him and it's shining through his eyes. Trystan grins at me.

"You are impossible. You do know that, right?" I'm breathing too hard, flustered beyond belief. Trystan loves it. I can see it in his eyes.

I dab and blend until the ugly marks around his neck are gone. They fading fast, but the colors are worse. Now there's an ample amount of green and yellow mixed with the blues and blacks. I finish his make-up and he stands and turns toward me. "I can't wait for tonight, for that scene that includes kissing you senseless on stage in front of dozens of people. I'm really looking forward to it."

I can't help it. The way he's looking at me makes me feel giddy. I slap his chest lightly. Trystan grabs my wrist and pulls me toward him, careful not to squeeze me too tight. "You would be—"

"So are you. I can see it in your eyes." I tear my gaze away from him, suddenly feeling very nervous. Trystan takes my chin and turns me back. "No one knows, love." He kisses my bottom lip. "They think we're acting." He kisses my top lip. "Only we know it's real."

CHAPTER 14

~TRYSTAN~

His heart is pounding. Mari is so close. Her lips are right there, but the bell is going to ring. Trystan settles for nipping her lip again. Mari slips off his lap and hands him another flannel.

"It'll help hide the marks if something happens to the make-up.

Besides, I like the way you look in it."

"In that case," Trystan reaches for the shirt and tugs it on over his black tee shirt. He leaves the front open. The collar makes him feel more secure. Mari knew it would. That's why she brought it for him. Trystan wants to say something, but words escape him. Instead he leans his forehead against hers for a second and looks into her eyes. "You're too good to me."

She smiles softly, shyly. It's like two people are living inside of her—one is so demur, but the other is a firework, bright and beautiful. "Come on. Today's going to be good. I can feel it." Mari backs away and reaches out for his hand, taking it in hers.

They walk up the metal stair case together. When they exit the auditorium, their hands separate. Trystan steps away a little bit, making things look like they've always been. No one suspects that he's fallen in love with this girl. No one knows they've spent a few nights together. No one knows how much he adores her, or how she makes him feel so alive that he's humming. No one knows anything and he likes it that way.

They head toward Trystan's locker, talking about the play later that night. Mari laughs at something he says and bumps him with her shoulder, taking hold of his arms and leaning into him. The contact makes him feel like he can fly. It jars other memories and he can almost taste her lip gloss.

That moment, that relaxed shared moment, is why he likes her. Mari never expects him to be someone else. She accepts him, scars and all. Trystan glances at her out of the corner of his eye, wishing he could cut class and spend the day with her. Last night wasn't enough. He can't ever get enough of her. When Mari isn't there, he burns for her. She's everything to him. They're walking and talking again. Trystan glances at her, reaches over and brushes the back of his hand against hers. She smiles up at him. His heart is soaring higher and faster than he ever thought possible.

But when they turn the hallway that leads to Trystan's locker, everything changes. That tender moment shatters. It's like Trystan is shoved out a window and is falling too fast to stop. There are tons of people at the other end of the hall. Trystan scans the crowd and sees Brie, Seth, and too many people to name. There's a woman dressed in a suit with a microphone. A man with a large camera on his shoulder stands with her. Tucker is standing to the side of the crowd, along with other faculty members. Everyone is buzzing like a happy mob.

Trystan's heart slams into his chest, thumping harder and faster. His breathing becomes jagged as his body tenses.

They know.

It's at that moment that Brie sees him. She flicks her eyes in his direction and hustles down the hall, sashaying in her tiny skirt. The swarm of people follow in her wake. Trystan's frozen in place. He considers running, but he can't because there's no way to hide from this. Dread chokes him, rendering him silent. The confident smile that usually lines his lips is long gone.

Brie steps into the space between Trystan and Mari and wraps herself around his arm. "This is Trystan Scott," she says beaming. He can feel her hand on his arm and hear her voice, but it sounds like static in his ears. She pulls him closer to the crowd, either that or they form a circle around him, surrounding him.

Trystan breathes hard, his eyes darting between the excited faces and the cameras. There's more than one. Trystan's heart lurches when he realizes that he's been cornered.

He reaches for Mari's hand, but she's gone. He can't even see her face. The crowd has swallowed him and she's gone.

Dread creeps around Trystan's throat like a noose, pulling tighter and tighter. These people know his secret. He can feel the icy cold truth racing through his veins. That means they know about the other night, about how his dad strangled him. Everything he's been trying to hide for so long is about to be exposed.

There's no way to stop it.

A voice cuts through the noise, through the chaos of his thoughts. The woman in the suit holds out the microphone to him, asking, "Are you Day Jones?"

SNEAK PEAK

Enjoy a free sample of the bestselling new adult romance series:

STRIPPED

A FERRO FAMILY NOVEL

CHAPTER 1

CASSIE

Bruce claps his big beefy hands at us like we're misbehaving dogs. "Come on ladies! Hustle! The bachelor party isn't going to be much fun if we never get there. Damn, Gretchen, you aren't even dressed, yet?"

She laughs like he's funny, even though Bruce is as far from funny as a person could get. He's the bouncer at the club and on nights like tonight, he comes with us to keep the guys from getting handsy. Some rich brat out on Long Island rented us for the night. There are seven of us going to perform on stage, plus the stripping wait staff, and dear, sweet, Bruce.

Gretchen is piling her long golden hair onto the top of her head and securing it with a long bobby pin. She's strutting around half naked, as if we like looking at her. She smiles sweetly at Bruce and waves a hand, bending it at the wrist like he's silly. "Please, I'll be ready before Cassie even finishes lacing up her corset."

She tilts her head in my direction as I fumble with my corset hooks. Every time I manage to hook one, another comes undone. Whoever invented the corset should be burned at the stake. The stupid thing might look cool once it's on, but getting into it is a whole other matter. Add in the fact that mine is a real corset—meaning it has steel boning—and breathing isn't something I can do either. I got this thing because it was authentic. I thought that meant it had period fabric or grommets or something cool. It turns out that authentic means metal rods built into the bodice, guaranteed to bruise my ribs. Fuck, I hate this thing, but I refuse to throw it away—it cost me three weeks' pay at my old job. Plus, it's not like I wear it every night. We only pull out the good stuff on holidays and for special events like this.

Bruce turns his head my way and looks like he wants to pull out his hair. I'm nearly dressed, except for this contraption. My ensemble includes the candy apple colored corset, lace-topped thigh highs, and a delicate little G-string, coupled with heels that could be used as weapons. If I ever get mugged wearing these shoes, you can bet your ass that I won't run, not that I could. These are the things I think about when I make my purchases. Can this purse do some damage? Maybe I should skip the leather Dooney and grab me that metal no-name bag with the sharp corners. My roommate and I live across the street from a drug den. Don't even get me started on that. I know we need to move, but knowing it and affording it are two different things. In the meantime, I buy accessories that can be used as weapons.

Glaring at her, I reply, "Gee, thanks, Gretch." My fingers push the next bit of metal through the grommet. This one stays put.

She bats her glittering lashes at me. "No problem." Gretchen is tall and lanky with a larger-than-life super model thing going on. I hate her. She's a bitch with a capital B. It's all good, though. She hates me, too. It's difficult to be hostile toward someone that likes you. Gretchen makes it easy to hate her guts.

Me, I'm not a supermodel. I'm nothing to look at—my mom drilled that into my head a million times. I'm completely average with sub-par confidence, but I can act. I can fake it so that once I hit that stage, I'm as good as the rest of the strippers.

No, I didn't dream of being a pole dancer when I was a little kid, but my life took some wicked turns and here I am, dealing with it. There are worse things I suppose, although I won't be able to think of a single one when I'm letting a bunch of pervs rake their lusty eyes over my naked body. The truth is, I hate this. I'd rather be anywhere else, doing anything else. The gynecologist's office, sign me up. Root canal, no problem. I'll be there early and with a smile on my face. Anything is better than this.

Bruce lingers in the dressing room for too long, staring at his watch. His thick arms are folded over his broad chest as he watches the second hand tick off the passing time. He ignores Gretch's gibe at me. I may be newer, but I pull in a lot more cash and that's what the boss likes—lots of money. As long as I keep doing it, I have a job.

I finally get my corset hooked up when Beth walks by. She's already wearing some frilly satin thing. "Hey, Cassie. Do you want me to lace you up?"

Tucking a piece of hair behind my ear, I nod. "Yeah, thanks." She laces me in, pulling each X tightly, cinching me up until I can barely breathe. "Tight enough?"

I try to inhale deeply, and can't because the metal bars inside the fabric won't permit it. I nod and press my hands to the bodice, feeling the supple satin under my hands. "Yeah, tighter than that and I'll pass out—or pop a boob."

She laughs, "You're the only one who worries about stuff like that. You're so cute." She ties off the strings and tucks them in before swatting my back when she's finished. My boobs are hiked up so high that I can't see my toes when I look down. I grab my robe and wrap it around me as we head to the cars. It's going to be a long night.

The ride to the party is short. We're on the north shore of Long Island, not too far from the coast. There are tons of old homes with huge lawns and even bigger estate houses nestled out of sight between towering oaks and pines. The place hosting the party looks like a castle. We pass through the gates and drive around to the side of the house. The van stops and we're told the usual—go wait in the servants' wing until it's time.

Beth and I walk inside, shoulder to shoulder, whispering about the garish wealth that's practically dripping from the walls as we walk inside. Gretchen and a few other girls trail behind us, chattering about what kind of tips they'll make tonight. A party like this can line a girl's pockets for a month if it goes well, but for me it'll do more than that. You see, I'm the main event, the mystery girl in the pink room—the bachelor's private-party dancer. While my coworkers are off in the main hall, I'll be earning the big bucks. That's the main reason why Gretchen hates my guts. Before I came along, she was the top stripper around here.

It's getting late, which means the party is well under way. Beth picks up a tiny sandwich off a tray as she walks to the back of the bustling room. "You think this guy knows what's coming?"

I shrug. "Like it matters, anyway? When's the last time we were sent away?"

"Uh, never." She pops the food in her mouth and chews it up.

I'm leaning against a counter top with my elbows behind me, supporting my weight. "My point exactly. Guys are dicks. They commit to marrying a woman, but this kind of crap the night before the wedding is okay." I roll my eyes as I make a disgusted sound, and straighten up. All of a sudden I'm talking with my hands and they're flying all over the place, "Tell me, why would a guy want a lap dance if he's in love? You'd think he'd only want his bride, but that never happens. He's always happy to have an ass in his face."

"Well, your ass is pretty awesome, or so I've heard." Beth smirks at me and glances around the kitchen. We're in the way, but there isn't anywhere else for us to go yet.

"Guys suck, that's all I'm saying."

"I know. You've said it a million times." She makes a *roaring* sound and shakes her fist in the air before turning to me and grunting, "Men. Evil."

"You're an idiot." I smile at her, trying not to laugh.

She points at me and clicks her tongue. "Right back at you, Cassie."

Bruce waves us over to the other side of the kitchen. "Cassie, Beth—follow me." We duck out behind him and follow the guy down the hall and slip into a little room. It's been done up in pale pinks with silver curtains, similar to the room I work in at the club. Since this is a party, Bruce added another dancer and I got to choose. While I work the stage at the front of the room, Beth will work the floor.

Bruce points a beefy finger at the stage and says to us, "Take your places, and remember that this client is the shit. Pull out all the stops, say 'no' to nothing. You got it?"

We nod in unison. The stage is elevated off the floor, with a few steps up at either end. It looks like the stage is new, built just for me. People usually rent those gray, make-shift stages that wobble when walked on, but not this guy. They spared no expense. The walls are lined with pale pink silks and illuminated from the floor. Clear tables flicker around the room with pink flames dancing within. It's seductive. The colors blend together, reminding me of pale flesh and kissable pink lips. As I climb the steps up the side of the stage and head to the silvery tinsel curtain, I call back to Beth. "Who is this party for again? And why is he the shit? I must have missed the memo."

She laughs as she's examining one of the lights within the glass table. It looks like fire, but it can't be since it's pink. She looks up at me. "Dr. Peter Granz, and he's the shit because he's a Ferro. Hence the swank party." Beth looks up when I don't answer.

I rush at Beth, nearly knocking her over. My jaw is hanging open as worry darts across my face faster than I can contain it. "Ferro?"

"Yeah, why?"

I'm in melt down mode. "I can't be here." I glance around the room and look at the door longingly. Before I make up my mind to run, I hear male voices approaching. Fuck! My heart pounds faster in my chest. If he's here, if Jonathan sees me—the thought cuts off before it finishes.

I'm ready to bounce out the window when Beth grabs my wrist and hauls me to the front of the room. She shoves me behind the curtain and hisses in my ear, "If you freak out now, Gretchen will steal your job. Snap out of it. Whoever this guy is, he isn't worth it."

The tinsel curtain in front of me flutters, but it conceals both of us for the moment. The male voices grow louder until the door is yanked open. The curtain rustles and I'm in full freak-out mode. He can't be here. He can't see me like this. At the same time, Beth's right. I can't skip out. Bruce will run me over with the van and there's no way in hell they'll ever give me another cent.

I stand there, frozen, unable to think. Every muscle in my body is strained, ready to run, but I don't move. My bare feet remain glued to the floor as I smash my lips together.

Then, I hear it—that voice. It floats through the air like a familiar old song. Oh God, someone shoot me. I can't do this. "You don't know what you're talking about. What guy wouldn't want a party like this?" Jonathan is talking to someone in that light, charming, tone of his.

"Uh, your brother, Peter. Do you know the guy at all? He's going to act like he loves it and get the hell out before you can blink." Glancing through the curtains, I can see the second man. He has dark hair and bright blue eyes like

Jonathan. The only difference is their posture. Jonathan has all his weight thrown onto one hip with his arms folded across his chest. The other guy's spine is ramrod straight, like he's never slouched in his life.

Peering at Jonathan through the tinsel, I see a perfect smile lace his lips. "Sean, I know him better than that. Pete is going to love this. It's exactly the kind of party I'd want if I was getting hitched."

"Yes, I know." Sean's voice is flat. He glances around the room with disgust, and slips his hands into his pockets. "Don't say I didn't warn you."

"Oh come on! It's Peter. What's he going to do?"

Sean laughs, like he knows something that Jonathan doesn't.

"Don't let that English teacher façade fool you, Jonny. He's as hot headed as I am. No one fucks with him. He's going to consider this a slap in the face, an insult to Sidney. Cancel the strippers before he gets here." Sean leaves the room without another word.

Jonathan Ferro lets out a rush of air and runs his fingers through his thick, dark, hair. The aggravated sound that comes out of his mouth kills me. I've heard it before, I know him too well to not be affected by it. That's the sound he makes when he knows he's screwed up, when he sees that he isn't the man he wants to be. There's always been this wall between Jonathan and his family. I guess he still hasn't gotten past it. Jon paces in a circle a few times and then darts out of the room.

"Holy shit." Beth looks at me and hisses, "What happened between you and him?"

It feels like icy fingers have wrapped around my heart and squeezed. I stare after him and utter, "Nothing, absolutely nothing."

CHAPTER 2

JONATHAN

Why does everyone think they know my brothers better than I do? I'm taking advice from Sean. How the hell did that happen? I'm walking swiftly down the long hallway, chin tucked, not watching where I'm going. The golden wallpaper appears to be glowing in the dim light. I run my hands through my hair and down my neck, and smack into someone.

When I look up, I'm ready to snap. "What the— Oh, it's you."

My closest friend, Trystan Scott, is standing in front of me. The guy is the brother I never had. He's not blood, but he might as well be called a Ferro because he's that loyal.

Trystan's wearing ripped jeans, a button down shirt with the top three buttons undone, and has way too much shit in his hair. "What the hell's going on? I thought the waitresses were supposed to be strippers. That was the coolest idea you've ever had. Imagine my disappointment when I rush out of rehearsal—away from the sexiest woman you've ever seen—and get here to find a bunch of chicks still wearing clothes." Trystan smirks and shoves his hands in his pockets.

I don't bother to answer him before resuming full speed down the hall. I have to find the guy from the club and cancel my awesome plan. Damn it, why does Peter have to be so difficult. Who doesn't want strippers at a bachelor party?

Trystan follows behind. "So, how's it going?" His voice has that teasing tone, which means he knows how well it's going.

"Nice hair," I throw back, and glance at him out of the corner of my eyes. Trystan makes a face and tries to smooth it down, but it doesn't move. "What'd they use, glue?"

His dark hair is sticking up all over the place. It looks like a porcupine toupee. "Something like that. I look like a fucking idiot."

"Yeah, but it's not the hair that does it—it's the make-up."

"Awh, fuck." Trystan swipes his hand across his eyes, trying to rub it off. "I forgot. I had somewhere to be—somewhere with strippers—so I ran over here as fast as I could." He smacks my arm with the back of his hand. "So, come on Jon, what's going on?"

"Apparently this isn't Pete's MO. I'm canceling the girls before Peter gets here. Sean said he'd bolt, that titties aren't his thing."

"Titties are his thing, but he prefers a certain pair." Trystan grins and looks over at me, pressing his hand to his chest. "The ways of the heart are—"

"And what would you know about that? You're a goddamn

legend. You've nailed every chick from coast to coast."

Trystan's smile brightens, but it's like there's something he's not telling me. Ever since I met him a few years ago, he's been like that. He doesn't talk about his past much, but I don't blame him. From the papers, I know Trystan's dad beat the shit out of him when he was a kid, but that's about it. The guy keeps to himself, but somehow manages to get pussy whenever he wants. A shy rock star is a fucking oxymoron, but the women fall at his feet. What do I know? Maybe I've been doing everything wrong this whole time. I shake the thoughts away and enter the main room.

The music pounds through the air, vibrating through me. The dim lights make it difficult to see the guy I'm looking for. He should be back in the kitchen right about now. I lean into Trystan. "I'll catch you later."

"Whatever you need, man." Trystan grabs my arm and squeezes. He's saying he's got my back, even if no one else does. The guy might be a train wreck, but he's good people under all that shit.

I slap his back, "Thanks. Catch you in a few. We can hit the bar after Pete gets here, because I'm not walking around sober if there's only guys here." Trystan laughs and agrees to get smashed with me later. You got to love the guy.

I weave through the crowd. There are already some strippers posing as wait staff. A woman with a tray and way too much make-up on her face brushes my side and turns toward me. "Champagne?"

Her cleavage is up to her neck and the thin white shirt she's wearing does nothing to hide the black bra underneath. Fuck, she's hot. I almost stop and flirt with her—almost—but I keep walking, because I'm not a total dick. This was supposed to be for Pete. I need to fix this before he gets here.

Sean falls in step beside me. "Tell me that I didn't see Scott at the bar?" Sean hates anyone who wasn't born with the name Ferro.

"Fuck off, Sean. He's my friend."

"He's using you." Sean's jaw is locked tight as he scans the crowd. "You're too naïve."

"You're an asshole." I'm not defending my friendship with Trystan or with anyone else. Sean acts like he knows everything, and he might be right most of the time, but he's wrong about Trystan. "The guy has his own millions. He doesn't need mine."

"He's unstable."

"You're unstable." I flick my eyes over to him.

Sean smirks. "Possibly."

"I can't chat about your mental health right now. I need to find the guy before all these girls rip their clothes off. Where's Pete?"

Sean laughs and points across the room. "He just got here."

"Fuck." I take off through the crowd, cutting through the guys, shoving some aside.

When I push through the kitchen doors, I see him. "Bruce! My man—change of plans."

Bruce is a huge guy and doesn't look pleased to see me. There are half dressed girls everywhere, slipping into their tear off waitressing outfits. Damn, this would have been so cool. Bruce has his thigh-thick arms folded over his chest. He glares at me. "No refunds."

"I'm not asking for one." I stand in front of the guy and feel like a toothpick, even though I'm not. Reaching into my pocket, I feel around for a hundred dollar bill. "I need them to keep their clothes *on*."

He gives me a weird look. "They're not supposed to be waitresses, Mr. Ferro. They're strippers and are expecting the tips that accompany the occupation."

Okay, I grab a fist full of bills and slip them into his hand. Bruce takes it and sees how much I've given him. I ask, "Maybe they could be waitresses for a couple of hours and then head out?"

"Maybe, but this isn't going to help the girls you hired for the private room. They're expecting tips, and if you cancel them out, they'll have left the club for nothing. You have to make good over there." The guy's voice is dangerously deep.

"Done. I'll go take care of it." I reach out and shake his hand.

As I turn to leave he clears his throat. "And if you'd like this kept quiet…"

I reach into my pocket and slap more cash into his fist. Bastard. The large man grins. "My lips are sealed, Mr. Ferro. A suggestion?" he asks, and I nod as my gaze cuts across the room to the clock. "Keep at least one girl in that private room for your guests. This is a party that people will talk about. You don't want them to think you're a pussy. You've got a reputation that people know about. They expect a little something extra at one of your parties."

"And you know this because…?"

"Because I've got ears, Mr. Ferro. Every man here is wondering what your big surprise will be this evening. You need to keep something for them, don't you?"

I don't answer him, because I know he's right. "Fine, I'll go speak to them. You keep the girls out here clothed."

Bruce laughs and leans back in his chair. "Done."

When I get back to the private room, I push through the doors without really paying attention until I hear a voice—that voice. It's like being hit in the face with a wall of cold water. Whatever thought I had in my head is gone. Wide eyed, I look up and scan the room. Two women are tangled together on the floor, fighting. Well, no they're not fighting, not really. I'm not sure what they're doing, and they have no idea I'm watching.

My heart pounds harder as her voice fills my head and I try to see her face. My body responds the way it used to—that hollow spot in the center of my chest aches, along with my cock. I stare in disbelief, watching two strippers wrestling on the floor, and stand in shock because one of them is Cassie Hale.

To ensure you don't miss any of
H.M. Ward's new releases, text
AWESOMEBOOKS to **22828**
and you will get an e-mail reminder
on release day.

MORE ROMANCE BOOKS BY H.M. WARD

THE ARRANGEMENT

SCANDALOUS

SCANDALOUS 2

SECRETS

THE SECRET LIFE OF TRYSTAN SCOTT

And more.

To see a full book list, please visit:

www.SexyAwesomeBooks.com/books.htm

CAN'T WAIT FOR H.M WARD'S NEXT STEAMY BOOK?

Let her know by leaving stars and telling her what you liked about SHATTERED in a review!

VIST H.M. WARD ON TWITTER:

www.Twitter.com/hmward

VISIT H.M. WARD ON FACEBOOK:

www.Facebook.com/AuthorHMWard

Made in the USA
Las Vegas, NV
02 February 2025

17418310R00121